THE PIRATE MUMS

JODIE LANCET-GRANT
ILLUSTRATED BY LYDIA CORRY

OXFORD
UNIVERSITY PRESS

Billy's family was not what you'd call **ordinary**.

When his friends came round for play dates, Billy's two mums loved to dance jigs and sing sea shanties.

Other families had cats or dogs—nice, *normal* pets.
Billy's mums had Birdbrain.

They insisted on using smelly old maps to find
their way on long car journeys . . .

. . . and their taste in house design was, well, **fishy.**

Billy just wished his family was a little more like everyone else's.

Which is why, when Mr Smart asked for parent volunteers to accompany his class on a trip to the seaside, Billy was horrified.

'Yo-ho-ho! I hear there's a boat ride too,' said Mummy. Billy's mums loved boats.

'Sounds like a right laaurrrrggghhhh,' said Mama. 'Count us in!'

Billy tried to make them change their minds.

He pretended
to have scurvy.

He hid Mummy's
favourite sailing hat.

He fibbed that the boat had
sprung a leak. But Mama said
she'd know just how to fix it.

Nothing worked.

Billy's mums just couldn't wait for the family
to sail the high seas together.

'Perhaps it won't be so bad,' Billy thought.
'Maybe no one will even notice how strange we are . . .'

'Er, no. You're not coming dressed like that!'
said Billy, on the morning of the trip.

'But we look right bonny!' protested Mummy.
'We'll be shipshape in this,' added Mama.

'Oh, please!' Billy exploded.

'Can't you be **normal?**

Just for today?'

'Oh. Erm, sure,' said Mama.

'Aye,' said Mummy. 'That be, erm, no bother, my little buccaneer, no bother at all.'

At the seaside, when it was time to board the boat, Billy took the first chance he got to dash off and join his friends.

'Anchors away!' Mama hollered as Captain Fishface set sail.

'Shhh!' whispered Billy.

The shore quickly faded into the distance.

'Oooh!' said the children, watching the seabirds swoop and soar above them.

'Wow!' they exclaimed, pointing at the quicksilver fish shimmering in the water.

It was Mama who noticed the sky change first.

'Shiver me timbers,'
Billy heard her mutter.

'Er . . . Mr Smart?' he called, pointing at the black clouds building on the horizon.

But Mr Smart hadn't quite found his sea legs, and was being seasick over the side of the boat.

All at once, the wind picked up speed.
The waves grew into giants.
Thunder rumbled.

BANG! A lightning bolt hit the boat and a mast came crashing down, ripping through every single sail.

If only there was someone else on board
who knew about boats . . .

'Mummy, Mama,' Billy whispered,
'I think we need your help.'

Billy's mums didn't need asking twice.
Mama fished a flare from her handbag
and set it off to grab everyone's attention.

'All right, me hearties!
First off, we need your coats.'

In a flash, the pirate mums expertly knotted the coats together . . .

. . . then tossed a corner to Birdbrain, who flew to the top of the one remaining mast and hooked on the makeshift sail.

The coats rippled in the breeze, but the boat stayed put.

'Never fear, mateys,' said Mummy.

'She just needs a little push off . . .

'A cannon aimed right at the water-line should see to that.

Which of you scallywags will help us pack it with flares?'

'Ready, aim, FIRE!'

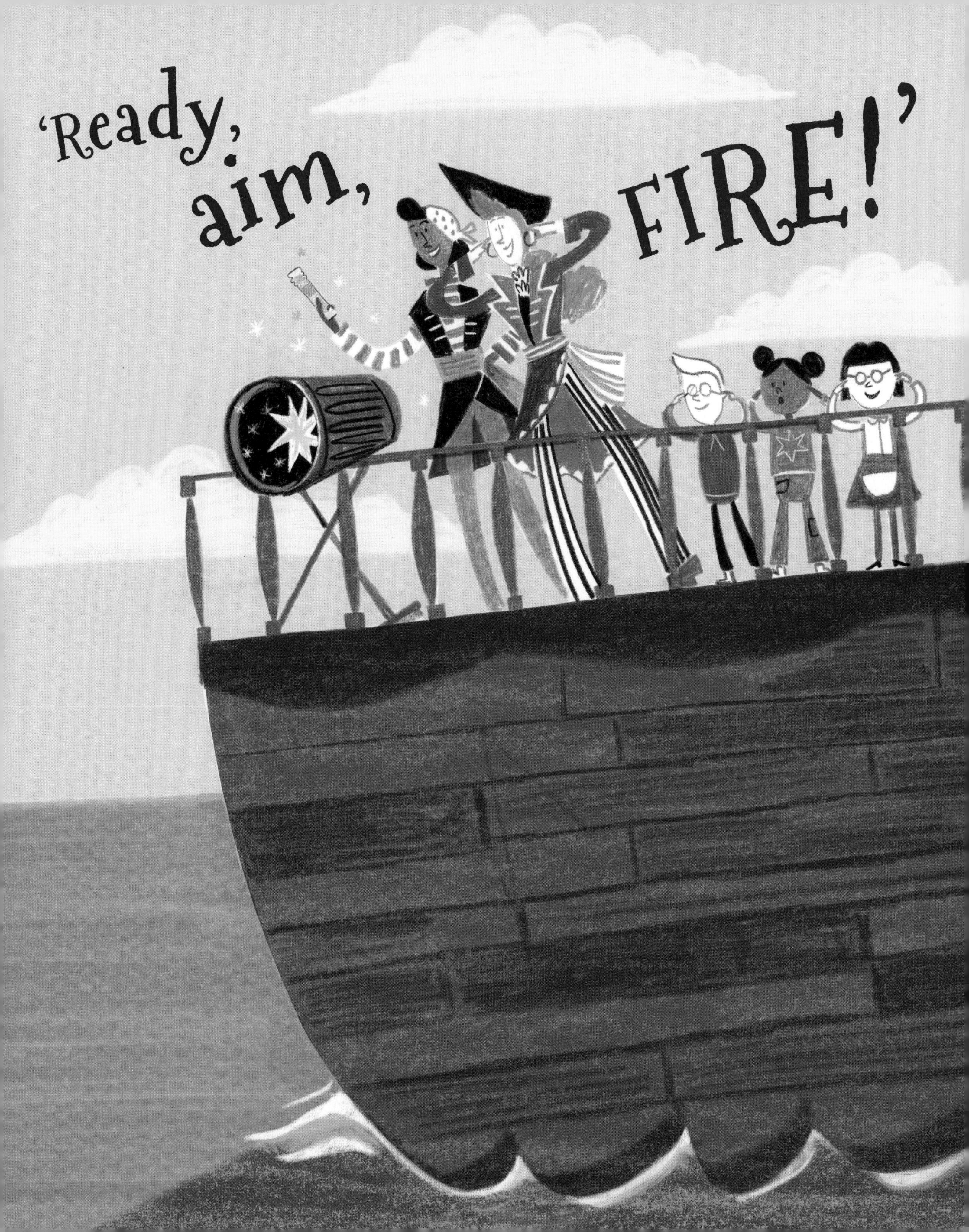

'Land ahoy!'
Billy shouted.

By the time Billy's mums had used Mama's cutlass to free Captain Fishface from his pongy prison, the boat was sliding into harbour.

'Bless Blackbeard's boots for your mums,' he said to Billy.

'They saved the day,' added Mr Smart.

'Oh-arr, that they
did!' agreed Billy.

'Who cares about ordinary?' thought Billy.

'It's a pirate's life for me.'